Finding Fulfillment
with
INTUISDOM

Finding Fulfillment
with
INTUISDOM

The Natural Path to Your Natural
Self in the Natural World

Anton Elohan Byers

iUniverse, Inc.
New York   Bloomington

Finding Fulfillment with Intuisdom
The Natural Path to Your Natural Self in The Natural World

iUniverse books may be ordered through booksellers or by contacting:

iUniverse
1663 Liberty Drive
Bloomington, IN 47403
www.iuniverse.com
1-800-Authors (1-800-288-4677)

Because of the dynamic nature of the Internet, any Web addresses or links contained in this book may have changed since publication and may no longer be valid. The views expressed in this work are solely those of the author and do not necessarily reflect the views of the publisher, and the publisher hereby disclaims any responsibility for them.

ISBN: 978-1-4401-8668-4 (pbk)
ISBN: 978-1-4401-8669-1 (ebk)

Library of Congress Control Number: 2009911145

Printed in the United States of America

iUniverse rev. date: 11/10/2009

"The finger that points at the moon is not the moon."

~Nagarjuna

This book is dedicated to the reader and to the prospect of everyone leading a richer, more fulfilling life and contributing to the lives of all others in so doing.

This book is also dedicated to the health of the planet and everything that lives on it and will live on it in the future.

Acknowledgments

I have always read the acknowledgments in books since I was a young child. To me it was like eating everything my mother prepared so carefully for my lunch, which I always ate without fail. I recognized then and I recognize now that authors want to express how much others have contributed to what they are trying to convey. Everyone I acknowledge here has provided energy and some kind of motivation to the overall message and they deserve respect and credit for it.

My wife Sierra has been solidly at my side during the times of frustration, the times of self doubt and the times of awakening. I could not imagine a more perfect love in all its imperfection, textures and extremes. No thank you would be big enough to fill the need I have to say it. Her laugh is as big as life is mysterious and with it she brings the joy of a child into each moment. She insisted her name not be listed as an author, because her fingers didn't do the typing, but her spirit is deeply rooted at the base of Intuisdom.

My mother Barbara was a critically important early role model who opened my young mind to what was really freethinking, and I sincerely don't know if I would have discovered myself without the door she helped open for me. I also acknowledge her for the exceptional art she brings into the world that inspires me every day.

My old friend Fred Glienna, whom I met and knew in my early teens, was one of the very, very few people in my life who practiced true mentorship, a lost art. His interest in my development and access to participation with what was going on around me demonstrated not only deep kindness, but also selfless investment of his energy in the world around him without any expected return. Whether I am conscious of it or not, I draw from my experiences through and with Fred's contributions to my life every day. To him go my undying thanks, appreciation and respect.

My sister Lauren, who was there at the time of greatest need. Through distance and time I will not forget.

The road has been very tough, but there have been many lights along the way: I give thanks, in chronological order of meeting them, to Fred Glienna, Terry Cooper, Hannah Lloyd, Lisa Cooper, Kathleen Edwards, Janet Evergreen, David Lott, Sharon Rosen, Laura Alden Kamm, Mikaela Quinn and Jim Ricker, Mel and Mary Rose (PhD), Paul Rose, Mari Tautimes, R.J. and Beverly Jordano, Joe Pascale and Karen Kuo, John and Lori Crippen, Charles Carter and Diane Aaronson, Don and Pam Teel, Bob and Kate Houston, Jerry and Dina Biesterfeld, Tom and Linda Pedacord and Paul and Carrie Mc-Minn. You each brought something important to my life that helped me come to this place, whether it was kindness, humor, sharing, wisdom, encouragement or just honest friendship.

Finally, let me thank the small team of people who willingly contributed to the book by sharing early reviews of it and helping to edit it. I give a very special extended thanks to the following people:

Sharon Rosen, my proofer, copy-editor and line editor. Sharon is a longtime friend whose intelligence and experience as a healer, teacher and writer contributed immensely to the review and editing process.

David Lott, an old friend who provided a review from the experienced mind of someone who actually works in the editing field on a daily basis and is himself a writer. His professional wisdom, encouragement and enthusiasm are deeply appreciated.

Mary Rose, a close and dear friend with a deep capacity for articulating from the source, whether that be in writing, teaching, speaking or singing. Her intelligence combines uniquely with her own drive for truth, and the results are often profound.

Mel Rose, a close friend and companion traveler, whose words are always chosen with the greatest of care from his natural self so he may give the most of himself to those around him.

And my wife Sierra again, for her earnest and thoughtful feedback. She took and offered the beautiful photo on the cover, and her dedication to the book and the process of writing it was and is of invaluable assistance, and I can only love her more for it.

Foreword

Over the course of our lives, my wife Sierra and I have both explored many, many avenues of possible explanation for the mystery of human life and ways to deal with the frustrations life brings—to perhaps find our own places of relative comfort and even a way to give back some of what we have learned along the way. Most of the typical religious, spiritual and intellectual (including academic) paths we found that already existed provided little meaning for us, though we did glean little bits here and there from those teachings. We looked at everything from traditional religions to shamanism to traditional Western social sciences to Hindu mysticism and various yoga practices and philosophies to teachings of channelers to eco-psychology and everything in between.

What we found was that whatever was underneath those teachings—whatever they were really trying to get to—tended to be obscured by the teachings themselves, so the validity of them was very difficult to experience. Either there was no validity, or that validity was twisted so completely from its point of origin that it became incomprehensible or it was simply being taught poorly.

We could not help but wonder why there were so many competing paths and why so little seemed to be understood about life. Many people *claimed* to know the answers, but there never seemed to be proof we could experience. Why are there *thousands upon thousands* of books that seem to contradict each other? Why, we asked ourselves, wasn't the answer all tied up in a ribbon and just handed to us?

In any case, it was when we finally gave up looking outward rather than inward that the answers and truths came. It was when we let it show up that the truth became apparent. We did not develop a new path as much as we simply observed the simple but powerful nature of reality (what we call the natural world), the mistakes we had made in perceiving it before and how we found our way to an appropriate and fulfilling relationship with the natural world as our natural selves. To communicate this we merely articulated our observations with a simple vocabulary to give enough shape to this new understanding so we could illustrate its essence. That's what this book is all about.

To be clear, Intuisdom doesn't reject the major religions or any particular religion or path, for that matter; however Intuisdom does deeply question the necessity of complex frameworks and teachings for an experience of profound connection, the opportunity for personal and spiritual development of the highest order and for access to personal roles in healing ourselves and our planet. If anything, Intuisdom should complement traditional religions.

Contents

"To be yourself in a world that is constantly trying to make you something else is the greatest accomplishment."

~ Ralph Waldo Emerson

Introduction

The word Intuisdom refers to an organic modality of personal and spiritual development that starts with the observation that access to ultimate truth, potential and connection to everything around us resides naturally within every individual. No complex external rules or teachings are necessary to experience this, find fulfillment in life and further develop ourselves to our highest capacities, other than basic instruction.

The first stage of Intuisdom is about discovering fulfillment through unlocking a fundamental blocking of our natural ability to perceive reality as it is. We start with a set of observations of what we need to understand and basic skills we need to develop to move forward as individuals to find fulfillment, opportunity and growth, whether that growth is personal, spiritual or both.

These observations function together as a simple model with each part synergistically working with the other parts, and with development in any of the parts affecting overall growth. In the end, Intuisdom is just the state of natural wisdom we achieve when we reach through the clutter between us and true reality, or, as we say it, become the natural self in the natural world.

This book is about the first and most critical stage of development through Intuisdom—that of finding fulfillment. This stage is comprised of five core observations we have labeled The Nature of Fulfillment, The False Self in the False World, The Natural Self in the Natural World, Becoming the Natural Self in the Natural World, and Engagement. Each of these observations covers a fundamental understanding and some contain useful exercises, actions or skills necessary to achieve the overall goal of fulfillment. A final chapter concludes the book with some tips to help you move forward.

This stage of the Intuisdom model is only a partial one as it only serves to bridge from a standard (false) model of reality to something beyond that. It will help give you that understanding and the basic tools to experience it for yourself, uncover the potentials that live inside it, and move forward. This should leave you the freedom to experience the nature of the world and your humanity on your own terms, without any particular expectations set for you.

Finally, let's make clear right here that this is a simple book because it has to be, because the heart of what it describes is simple. It will not take long to read and should not take long to understand. It is our deepest intention to convey in short order what we could not ourselves find so simply put and spare you the years it took us to discover these truths. There is a small glossary at the back of the book to help you with definitions for the tiny vocabulary of terms we use here, as we use words you may already know with your own definition and a few you probably don't know at all. Some of these words are essentially interchangeable and some need clear definition for the way we specifically mean them.

So, let's get to it!

"The major problems in the world are the result of the difference between the way nature works and the way man thinks."

~Gregory Bateson

Chapter One:
The Nature of Fulfillment

Of all of the human needs beyond the basic survival needs of food and shelter, fulfillment is probably the most fundamental and satisfying. Finding meaning in what we choose to do in our daily lives as well as over the duration of our entire lives gives us the richness of experience and the fertile ground in which to plant the seeds of the next step while still getting the most out of the present.

However, many people find it terribly difficult to find fulfillment, even in small measure. After all, where do we even start? It seems that frustration is everywhere—in personal opportunity and performance, unlocking our potential, money, relationships, spirituality, jobs, health or understanding life in general. Not much seems to provide stable footing for a sense of potential growth toward something meaningful, and those hopes we do have turn out too often to be hollow. It's as if we are living in a dream in which nothing connects, we never reach the top of the stairs, we never find the right door, and the object of our affections always remains one step ahead of us.

The obvious—though incorrect—conclusion that most of us come to every day is that fulfillment is not for us, that we have missed out, that we are not smart enough or educated enough or pretty enough or rich enough or holy enough or lucky enough. This conclusion stops us cold in our tracks and only isolates us further from the truth and the potential that lies behind it.

Another incorrect conclusion is that we simply haven't worked hard enough yet, that if we keep grinding away using ordinary expectations and understandings of how to operate in life we will eventually make it to the "promised land."

Fulfillment, however, does not come from achievement within the standard model of reality. The lack of fulfillment is, therefore, not the result of failing to achieve within that same model.

Here's the key: **Fulfillment is a natural human response to participation in the natural world as the natural self once we leave behind the false self in the false world.**

We live lives that are terribly crippled by a critical mistake in the way we perceive ourselves and what is around us. We mistake what we have been told we are, what we believe we are, for what we really are. Once we allow our natural self to take over and begin to act as the natural self in the natural world, everything else falls into place.

"The only way to find the limits of the possible is by going beyond them to the impossible."

~Arthur C. Clarke

Chapter Two:
The False Self in the False World

What gets in the way of fulfillment, potential and all the growth that goes with it is that we incorrectly believe that abstractions about reality *are* reality. We hold on to these abstractions—thoughts, images, symbols, beliefs, values, rules, measurements, expectations and so on—as if they themselves are us and the world around us. This creates a false self in a false world that we mistake as real, though they are *held in place only by us holding on to them, not by their truth.*

From the moment we are born, we live our lives in a swarm of abstractions that are dictated to us by the culture around us. We can easily become dizzy just considering how many different ways the false world lures us into believing it and what it tells us about our selves. Even a partial list bounces around from words to beliefs, ideas to equations, money to time, descriptions to illustrations, technologies to systems, messages to metaphors, signs to symbols, rules to roads, news to laws and even our cherished cars and homes (which are abstractions of our selves and our personal space). We take these to be all of reality; in fact, we are *told* they are reality.

We then take these abstractions and use them as our tools of perception, our lenses for experiencing, communicating and learning about reality, how to maneuver within it and our relationship with it. Abstractions become our primary perceptual mode. When we want to know where we are, we look for the sign to tell us. When we want to know what we are supposed to do, we look for instructions. When we want to know who we are supposed to be, we ask people around us. When we want to know how well we have done, we look at our report cards.

Here's the key: **The false self in the false world is a constellation of abstracted thoughts, ideas, values, expectations, possibilities, technologies, beliefs, and so on that we mistake for reality. It therefore sets an artificial limit for what we as individuals can do within our lives, what we can experience, how much we can grow, what we will try to do and not try to do, in what ways we can grow, what roles we can fill, what we can contribute, how much connection we have with natural rhythms and whether or not we can find fulfillment and meaning. These abstractions are both the fabric of the false self and the false world and the perceptual mode through which the false self perceives reality.**

Mind Trap

The fundamental problem appears to start with an unfortunate dysfunction of the human mind—mistaking abstraction for reality—and thus the false self in the false world is born. Attempting to understand this from a psychiatric, psychological, religious, cosmological or any other kind of analytical process or framework is a complete waste of time—this is just a mistake we make in the way a cat will mistake a fake mouse for a real one, even when the cat in some way appears to understand that it is not real. For the cat it's no big deal, but for us it is a huge problem, whether we are conscious of it or not.

The mind of the false self is a fascinating thing. The mind appears to be capable of amazing feats; however, it can make serious and dangerous mistakes of perception. Encouraged by the culture around it, the mind very readily becomes a machine of abstraction: at best, it detects patterns, abstracts those patterns into "fixed" values and then mistakes those values to be reality itself; at worst, it simply takes what others have told it is real to indeed be real without much question or verification at all. If we take the perceptions of the false self at face value, we are then forced to live within the confines of its abstractions and within the measures of its dimensionless world.

Over time, the many forms of this mistake start to knit themselves together into a false reality built from thousands upon thousands of abstractions. This eventually becomes a worldview, an adopted and relatively comprehensive fabrication that appears to be real. After all, everyone else tells us it's real so it must be, right?

Think back in your own life to a time when you discovered something was possible you didn't think was possible. It could have been a magic trick, a woman becoming a CEO of a major corporation, an engineering feat using extremely simple techniques, a man changing an animal's behavior by behaving differently toward it instead of disciplining it, a tree growing from another tree or suddenly understanding something you were sure you didn't have the capacity to understand. The most obvious reason you didn't know these things were possible is because *you believed they were impossible.* These examples may seem mundane, but don't miss how important the implications are for what else may be possible that you currently think is impossible.

Communication and Learning with Abstraction

Let's be clear about how we define what an abstraction is. We define anything that is a reference to something else, but is not that thing itself, as an abstraction. The mind is exposed to this in many forms, but the most obvious and the most pervasive abstractions we encounter on a daily basis are words. A brief study of how we use words and language demonstrates that the false self not only mistakes abstractions for reality, but also must process abstractions in sequences in order to communicate with them or learn their meaning, sequences that are fraught with problems.

In all written languages, there is a sequential nature to the abstractions we call words (or symbols). In spoken language there is more versatility, but words are modified by certain rules set out for each language to help indicate the relationship of the words to each other and the overall meaning of a sentence (e.g. which is the subject, which is the object, etc.). These systems for teaching and learning imply there is distance and time in experiencing and learning, distance and time we cannot escape.

Sentences are constructed of words that each have a multitude of meanings and relationships with each other. They are constructed by the writer or speaker and then deconstructed by the reader or listener to hopefully find the inner meaning. This process is not only extremely time consuming, but it also can lose immense amounts of meaning through the multiple stages it goes through to finally be digested. And we mistakenly take this process and all the associated abstractions that accompany it as our primary method of communicating and learning.

Potential Lost

Mistaking abstraction for reality, perceiving through abstraction, and attempting to learn and grow through sequential processes of constructing and deconstructing language all hide potential. That is to say, these problems so disconnect us from reality and what is real that we miss what is real because we are busy believing something else.

Simply put, we don't try to do what we don't know is possible, and if we mistake abstractions (remember that abstractions include beliefs, values, expectations and so on) for reality we never attempt to step outside those abstractions, and therefore can't find the parts of us and the world they have excluded.

The net result of this is that potential is only uncovered accidentally or by incrementally eating away at the edges of what we think we are, and our lives suffer tremendously for this.

Illustration exercise:
The Sentence of Disappearing Potential

I discovered this simple illustration years ago when I was trying to figure out how to re-write sentences and paragraphs that didn't seem to come out right the first time. It's an extremely revealing illustration of the mental mechanics that keep us inside the false self in the false world.

Read the following sentence and quickly mentally fill in the first few words that come to you for the blank spot at the end of the sentence:

The cat caught a _____.

What did you come up with? The cat caught a bird? The cat caught a mouse? Not too original, right? Okay, maybe you immediately thought of something creative, but whatever you came up with was caught and caught by a cat.

Let's try it again with this:

The cat _____.

What did you come up with this time? The cat played with a toy? The cat jumped off a roof? The cat ran up a tree?

And, finally, let's try this:

The _____.

Well, you get the point. Each time we remove specific context and assumptions by removing words, the potential opens up. What was fixing you to the original sentence and forcing you to maintain some kind of imaginary continuity? Nothing, actually. You only assumed the sentence was fixed to a certain point and that the remaining potential was limited by that.

An interesting twist to this illustration shows how the tiniest of changes can close down our potential. Let's go back to the first example sentence. This time there is no trickery and you must write down things that fit into the sentence as written. Do the exercise one more time and quickly write down a list of five things the cat could catch.

The cat caught a _____.

I can almost guarantee that the items of your list all start with a consonant, simply because you were probably adhering to the rule in English that the article "a" precedes words starting with consonants. My poor example cat can't catch anything that starts with a vowel!

What is trapping us is our adherence to the abstractions we assume to be real. We take our cues about reality from what we are presented with, usually without question. In this case each partial sentence *seemed* to limit in one way or another what could be conveyed in the sentence. But that limitation was false.

I discovered that when I had truly gotten lost in my writing I often needed to erase the entire sentence or paragraph to let what really needed to come out not get trapped in what I had thought was supposed to come out or had tried before. None of the natural self or potential is trapped behind anything stronger than these flimsy assumptions.

Simple Exercise:
The False Self vs. the Natural Self

Take two sheets of blank paper and lay one on top of the other. On the top sheet, take a long time to write everything good and bad about yourself, how you measure up, how you fail, why you have failed, why you have succeeded, what your hair color is, what your weight is, what your IQ is, what your job is, what your ambitions are, what your age is, crimes you've committed, wrongs that have been done to you, relationships you have and have had, how much education you've had, and so on, until every last drop of what you know about yourself is on that top paper. Go ahead and write in the little spaces that are left—just don't write on the bottom sheet. Continue reading when you are done.

When you are all done, look at that top sheet as a totality of you and take it in for a few minutes. Now, lift up just the corner of the sheet to see what is underneath. Wow, a blank page. Now put the top sheet back over the bottom sheet for a minute and consider the layer of blank page underneath with a layer of everything you know about yourself on top. Now, remove the top sheet and safely burn it or destroy it, leaving the blank sheet. (If you are worried about destroying some of what you are symbolically, realize that whatever is really you will always be really you; it can't be folded, spindled or mutilated.) So, what's left? Just the you that is waiting to emerge.

Now, before we leave this exercise, let's consider the blank page one more time. Is it empty or just not marked on with symbols that reflect, *but aren't*, you? It is really just what it is, with all its potential intact and ready.

"Only in the last moment of human history has the delusion arisen that people can flourish apart from the rest of the living world."

~Edward O. Wilson

Chapter Three:
The Natural Self in the Natural World

The Natural Self

When we strip away the abstractions, the false self that we have held as real for so many years and the so-called primary senses of touch, taste, smell, sight and hearing, what is left? At first, nothing at all seems to be left; but as we relax into this nothingness we begin to become aware that it has its own properties, chief amongst them a deep fertility. What remains may be thought of as a purer state or a simpler mode of experiencing, but it is a critical one to achieve to find fulfillment and everything that lies beyond fulfillment. Welcome to the natural self.

Once we are beyond perceiving just these basic properties of experience that lay underneath the false self, we start to sense shapes, flows and rhythms. And even more importantly, we begin to sense potentials and opportunities, the aspects of the natural self and the natural world that beg to be enjoyed and brought into our lives with action. Indeed, these aspects of the natural world are actually shared with the natural self, and their presence within the self brings us to the realization that there is deep common ground between us and the outside world.

The natural self is fertile, expansive, connected, dynamic, subtle, emerging. The natural self is what shows up when the false self is gone.

Perceptual Mode of the Natural Self

The natural self experiences neither abstractions nor the processing required to distill meaning from abstractions. It experiences through *resonance* and learns through *emerging awareness*. While the false self experiences abstractions in place of reality, the natural self experiences reality *by being part of it*. The natural self learns by observing the shapes and flows moving through it and allowing them to emerge into consciousness.

This perceptual mode is deeply informed by natural rhythms around us and through us if we allow it. The natural self resonates with these rhythms and we find our place within them.

In the next chapter we will define the perceptual mode of the natural self more fully and discuss the primary methods of orienting to it.

The Natural World

The natural world is the world as it is after the false world has been recognized; at the very least a vast and probably indefinable stretch of something that is far more dimensional and interconnected than space or time as we are taught to perceive them. It contains a subtle symphony of rhythms and flows we are extremely isolated from in the false world.

The false world creates a small, distorted pocket within that vastness that is definable because we have made it abstract by the very act of defining it. Envision the false world as a small, hollow egg we live within, thinking that the inside of the shell is everything that defines the world, everything that defines what we can and can't do, can and can't be, can and can't feel. The natural world is everything without abstraction.

The Relationship Between the Natural Self and the Natural World

It is very important to understand that the natural self is an extension of the natural world. As such, it is simply an instrument of localized consciousness, an organ of expression of the natural world. The rhythms and cycles that flow through the natural world also flow through the natural self and inform it of where it is, what it is and what its relationships are. As you use the simple practices included in the next chapter, you will find that the natural self is a dynamic conduit through which consciousness is experienced at whatever level you allow it.

The natural self and the natural world sit nested together and function as parts of the same whole. If the natural world were a mountain, the natural self would be a river flowing from it. If the natural world were a patch of earth, the natural self would be a flower rising from it. If the natural world were a star, the natural self would be its light.

*"…The sage is guided by what he feels
and not by what he sees…"*

-Lao Tzu

Chapter Four:
Becoming the Natural Self
in the Natural World

At this point in the book we have softened the hold the false self in the false world has on you by making you aware of its existence as falsely representative of what reality really is. But you will begin to experience the natural self more fully as you orient your moment-to-moment perceptual mode to it. With the practices of exploring resonance, recognizing emerging awareness, single-point meditation and exposure to natural rhythms, you will start to actually shift into the natural self as your primary mode of perception.

Resonance

Resonance is one of the two primary aspects of the perceptual mode of the natural self. It is how we sense what is real and what is not. Resonance is the sensation of something existing that is not accessible by your other senses. It might help if you think of resonance as the first sense instead of a sense that exists *after* the so-called primary senses.

Active and Passive Resonance

Just as with your other senses, there are different components to resonance and to developing your use of it, starting with two main types, active and passive. Active resonance is defined by the conscious intention of putting it into motion, of consciously using it to learn how it works, as well as to achieve glimpses of your natural self. Passive resonance is achieved when enough blocks are removed from your moment-to-moment experience and what comes through you from the natural world does so primarily of its own accord.

Active Resonance

Active resonance is practiced by simply sending your awareness through your own body as if it were a small wave of water that starts at the top of your chest and moves quickly to the base of your pelvis. Just practicing active resonance is beneficial, as it brings a heightened consciousness of what your body feels like, something many of us completely ignore. But what we are really seeking here is the occasional "bounce-back" that comes back to our awareness, a sign that something is there you weren't aware of.

At first, the bounce-backs just provide location information—where in the body you feel it—but as you get better at it, other aspects of what you are sensing will show up and you will become aware of the nature of whatever it is. It could be something that needs to be released (e.g. particular abstractions) or it could be an aspect of the underlying structures or dynamics of the natural self or natural world.

Now, once you start to sense these things your first response is often to try to attack this curiosity you have discovered within yourself by analyzing it. Using what you will learn from meditation, let this impulse go. Once you have made direct contact with your natural self, it will start to release itself into your consciousness and experience. This is one of the most beautiful aspects of this path—that once the doorway is opened by your own actions, the natural self will begin to reveal itself more and more actively and then the natural world will begin to reach through that natural self into your experience.

Confirming

Confirming is simply checking what you have found or observed using resonance by letting the sensation disappear and repeating the process. Finding the same feeling again lets you know there is something legitimately there. Once again, the act of confirming is not about attempting to analyze what you found—just acknowledge it and it will begin to take care of itself.

Passive Resonance

Passive resonance is simply the awareness of what you are, what your potential is, what your relationship to reality is, what the nature of reality is and what is passing through you without abstraction. It is experienced across a spectrum of quantity and quality, from little bits to torrents, from things that don't make any particular sense to things that are deeply meaningful. A bit is just a small piece of a specific awareness that appears in your consciousness, while a torrent is a huge stream of awareness that may erupt within you like an eloquent and extemporaneous poem, beautiful, concise and unquestionably real.

Emerging Awareness

At some point resonance transitions from feeling something to consciously knowing something about the nature of reality without using cognitive processes. This can appear to happen spontaneously or it can come in stages. The appearance of emerging awareness is the endpoint of resonance and the defining point of moving into the natural self in the natural world.

A warning, however: If emerging awareness illustrates a profound and life-changing new understanding while you are driving on the Long Island Expressway, do not attempt to write it down or text it to your significant other! One of the most important features of truth is that it is always there. It will come back to you, don't worry.

There isn't much else that needs to be said about emerging awareness—you'll know it when it shows up!

Here's the key: **Resonance and emerging awareness are the primary aspects of the perceptual mode of the natural self. It is useful to practice resonance actively at first, but it will become simply a way of life after some time. Emerging awareness is the conscious recognition of the nature of reality by the natural self.**

Meditation

One of the most fundamentally important exercises you can do toward becoming your natural self in the natural world is a form of single-point meditation. This exercise immediately allows you to distinguish the false self from your first conscious experience of the natural self; through practice, you learn to further release the false self to become more and more the natural self.

Keep in mind that you are already your natural self—that the false self only obscures it. This means that meditation is only orienting you to what already is, rather than taking you somewhere else.

Now, we have told you that this practice is simple and that it is about orienting you to your natural self, but we need to spend just a moment to distinguish this style of meditation from so many others by being clear about what Intuisdom meditation is *not*.

Intuisdom meditation is not about peace, love and happiness. It is not about imagery, colors or better places. It is not about holiness, angels or guides. It is not about life lessons, plans from before you were born or past lives. It is not about hope, prayer, belief or faith. Intuisdom doesn't necessarily reject anything specific about the above lists, but opening the doorway to the natural self must be done with a minimum of abstractions and a maximum of direct experience.

It bears repeating one more time that Intuisdom meditation is about orienting to your natural self; and when this occurs, the natural self begins to allow the natural world into your experience, and you and it emerge together. The focus is on opening the door, not what might come through it. When you open the door, it will come to you.

Exercise:
Intuisdom Meditation

Now, before we begin:

Find a relatively quiet place to sit that is free from normal distractions and where you know you can keep quiet for at least 20 minutes (no TV's, phones, etc.). Sitting on the floor or ground with a cushion for your posterior will be best, but using a chair or sofa is fine, as long as you are not tempted to mistake this new state you will discover as time to go to sleep!

Your posture should be relatively straight, with the spine and head erect, but the body relaxed. Allow your hands to rest comfortably in your lap—you might even use a pillow on your lap during meditation to rest your forearms and hands if you find your back hurting after meditating a few times. Breathing should be done with the diaphragm fully engaged so that the belly distends on your in breath.

Close your eyes and allow your thoughts and other abstractions to dissipate. You may at first use your breath or some other internal physical sensation as a focal point, but eventually your focus should be the space between thoughts and other abstractions. This space *is your first glimpse of the natural self* and is what you are aiming directly for. At some point this will become your comfort spot, the place you go naturally, even if it takes a little more time on some days than on others. This is your doorway to your natural self.

Allow the thoughts and abstractions to come and go, never pushing them away, just letting them float away or even just be. A dog barking outside, for instance, is just what it is and nothing more. Even an itch will go away if you bring your focus back to the natural self. Bring your focus back to the space between the abstractions…again and again.

When you are done with your meditation, you can write down what you experienced, if you wish, but try to avoid over-analyzing it and therefore making what shows up too abstract. What is real will always be there—allow it to be. I personally have immense amounts of notes I jotted down after meditations, but I almost never read them after they are initially written (more on this later in the chapter on engagement).

Meditating is helpful even if you can only do it for five minutes at a shot, but try for a minimum of twenty minutes at first and gradually work your way to an hour or more if you have the time. If you can't do it every day, just do it as you can—but return to it. Your progress toward your natural self has everything to do with how much you put into it. It can be very slow and it can be very quick—it is up to you.

"I Can't Meditate"

We hear this so often it's almost funny, but it's not. This mistaken notion keeps people from using meditation as the powerful tool it is and what can come from it. It's a bit like saying, "I can't lift weights because I am not strong enough."

When we ask people what they mean by this, they almost always say something like, "I always start thinking about something or find something uncomfortable about my body or a noise that keeps me from concentrating." In Intuisdom, meditation is the practice of allowing abstractions to dissipate from your consciousness, leaving only the natural self. It is not the practice of being able to be completely clear of abstraction all the time. It is about recognizing the false self attempting to reassert itself and redirecting your perceptions back to the natural self over and over.

Here's the key: **Intuisdom meditation is about orienting to the natural self by recognizing abstractions (the false self and the false world) and allowing them to dissipate. If you are practicing this process over and over you are meditating, despite how many times the abstractions return. Meditation is not a perfect state.**

Natural Rhythms

As we have said several times already, becoming the natural self in the natural world happens through orienting to its perceptual mode. A critical aspect that underlies and informs this perceptual mode is our connection to the natural world around us.

The fact that we are ambulatory seems to confuse us into thinking that we are separate from the earth, but we are very far from separate. We are as connected as any tree, flower, ant, mountain stream, lichen, season of change or ripple of wind. We are part of the whole. We don't mean this metaphorically or in the assumption that everyone feels a kinship with the earth—we mean that we are actually connected to the world around us in deep and important ways, whether we are conscious of it or not. Working with these connections can be a valuable part of your growth as they help align your natural self with the natural world, making resonance simpler and clearer. This, in turn, brings meaning to the rhythms you become aware of and informs the natural self.

Think for a minute about what your body is composed of. It is built of transient pieces of the rest of the universe: specks of dirt, stone and bone; pieces of fish and fowl; water from the deepest seas and the wildest rivers. It is literally composed of elements that were forged in the hearts of stars and danced through time and space to become part of you.

Any rhythms that involve nature as it is without human interference are useful, but we start with the elementals of earth, water, air and fire as these are what our bodies are made of and interact with in every moment. It's not important that we understand intellectually how this happens or understand it in any analytical way—it is important that we experience the rhythms and let our bodies do the rest.

The lives we lead in the false world along with everyone else isolate us from these rhythms and even replace them with rhythms from the false world. As just a small example, the false world tends to abstract the rhythms into four seasons of fairly fixed meaning, but the reality of the natural world is vastly more integrated and interactive, with seasonal rhythms never being anything absolute. There is a season in every moment that is deeply related to everything else, deeply expressive of everything else and deeply important to the natural self in its place within the natural world.

Exposure to natural rhythms can happen in a myriad of ways, from smelling grass and dirt, to listening to ocean waves or dripping water, to listening to the chirping of birds or insects, to watching a flower unfold, to resting your gaze lightly on a hillside of trees subtly moving in a light wind. Choose whatever is available to you at the moment, whatever is close by, wherever you are. What is important is that we take time to be a part of it, and to allow the natural self to align with it.

Just as with meditation, you can choose to write down notes about your experiences with natural rhythms, but try to keep your notes simple. Let the experience come through the natural self

Here's the key: **Natural rhythms and flows are an extremely important part of the natural world. They connect the natural self to the natural world through our experience of them. They both help us align to the natural self through being exposed to them and inform us of who we are and where we are.**

"Your work is to discover your work—and then with all your heart to give yourself to it."

~Prince Gautama Siddartha

Chapter Five:
Engagement

At this point we have discovered where the answer really is—inside, not outside. We may even have begun orienting to the natural self. However, discovering the natural self and the potential it opens doesn't do that much for us if we do not activate it by engaging with what we have discovered. For some of us, this suggestion may be very difficult to swallow; after all, this is why we wanted the freedom from the false self to begin with—to snuggle down inside ourselves and go to sleep after we discover a nice little morsel of fulfillment! However, Intuisdom is not just uncovering the natural self, but also allowing it to participate as a flow from the natural world through the natural self back out into the natural world.

As we have stated, the natural self exists to express the natural world. The stage of growing that starts with leaving behind the false self and discovering the natural self is continued by engaging the world with your newfound potential and deep connection. Fulfillment is simply a little bonus that comes with this development and activation.

Expressing

Writing down or talking about what you are experiencing can be the beginning of engagement, as these are acts of bringing through what has erupted within you into the world around you. There are two points of concern, however.

As you may have noted in the illustration of disappearing potential, sometimes writing things down can appear to exclude potential, so write without attachment to what you are writing—give it space to grow. Write to allow what is unfolding to be articulated, but don't mistake what you are writing for the manifestation itself. Even this book is not the awakening that is now happening within you—it is only an articulation of a path to get there.

As well, recognize that your movements toward change in your life may be resisted by others. It is best to speak your truth when it has more fully developed within you.

Engaging the World

Where to start the larger scope of engaging is an open question. It depends entirely on what is showing up in you at the time. If, for example, the natural self first starts to develop a sense of heightened compassion, allow that to express outwardly to those around you. If you find that you have let go of certain emotional burdens, allow that freedom to let you become more active in relationships. If you find that you have become more grounded and stable during dramas going on around you, allow that stability to guide your own choices about participating in those dramas. If you discover that you have a previously unnoticed interest in something, start actively working on it. We could go on and on with this, but you should get the point by now.

Here's the key: **Engagement is what actually triggers fulfillment, and fulfillment is the carrot that brings you to leave behind the false self and recognize the natural self. Engagement is the final step in aligning the natural self with the natural world and is the primary act of living in the natural world as an expression of it.**

The flower engages by opening. The river engages by flowing. The star engages by shining. And you engage by participating in the natural world as your natural self.

"Is it so bad, then, to be misunderstood? Pythagoras was misunderstood and Socrates, and Jesus, and Luther, and Copernicus, and Galileo and Newton—and every pure and wise spirit that ever took flesh. To be great is to be misunderstood."

~Ralph Waldo Emerson

Chapter Six:
Distractions on the Path

As you orient more and more to the natural self, how and why you were fooled by the false self and the false world will become more apparent, but let's give you a head start by identifying some important stumbling blocks that can work toward slowing your development. These blocks include the attitudes of people around you, your own self-righteous justifications and the false world trying to keep you in the fold.

Other People

You grew up surrounded by people and you live your life today surrounded by people. Many of these people helped imbue you with your identification as the false self, though they were not consciously aware of it.

Unfortunately, most of the people on the planet have no useful experience with the natural self and the natural world. Because of this it is easy to blame them for contributing to your situation, but such blame would miss the point of becoming your natural self.

Allow others to be what they are as you move through your re-orientation and place your focus internally. The source of virtually all of your frustration and lack of development is simply in the misidentification of the false self as real, not other people's actions.

Justification and Distraction

Hatred, anger, annoyance, irritation, frustration, worry, fear, dismay, displeasure, pain, sorrow, embarrassment, jealousy and desire are all different kinds of abstractions that become distractions that allow you to justify your failure to develop or be fulfilled by blaming something or someone else. This is simply a way of telling yourself that you can't get beyond something because of something you can't control. Whether the cause of this apparent lack of control is yourself, someone else, an inanimate object, an institution, a philosophy, a rule, a sound, a color or a smell matters not at all. The cause of the distraction, the distraction itself and whether you can claim it is justified or not are all just properties of the same thing. They are merely distractions that remove your attention from your natural self as it exists in the natural world.

Justifying your distraction of choice is simply a habit. There may be good reasons to perceive that something external caused something you find uncomfortable in your life, but these things *don't* stop you from being your natural self, and this is the goal—don't forget that.

We tend to get lost when we paint the world as something inherently positive or negative that we don't control, but does control us. And then we become waylaid, our efforts lost in our blame.

Move back to the natural self and move on.

"Help, the false world is chasing me!"

The false world does have its own dynamics and an artificial life of its own, but they are not worth more than a brief discussion here, as an elaborate discussion would only serve to slow your journey and nothing more. You should know that you are more useful to the false world if you play by its rules and there can be consequences for not playing by them. The false world may try to penalize you for changing your mind about what you want to do with your life or how you see and interact with the world, and you may hear the false world speaking through people you know and love.

The reach of the false world appears extraordinary—it seems as if it is all around you. But it isn't. It is only around you as much as you choose it to be. *You have the choice* of what to read, what to eat, who to be friends with, how to relate to others, how to spend your free time and *how you perceive reality*. You even have choice over your career, whether you are presently early on in your work life, later on or even retired.

Coexisting with the false world is simple, if not easy. It is the recognition of the false world and the false self and the orientation to the natural self that is your guide.

As someone wise once said to me about the false world, "be in it, not *of* it." At the time I didn't know then what she meant by that or how I might accomplish it, but now I do—and I hope you do, too.

"A human being is part of a whole, called by us the 'Universe,' a part limited in time and space. He experiences himself, his thoughts and feelings, as something separated from the rest—a kind of optical delusion of his consciousness. This delusion is a kind of prison for us, restricting us to our personal desires and to affection for a few persons nearest us. Our task must be to free ourselves from this prison..."

-Albert Einstein

Coda

As you read through this book you may have noticed that not everything is fully explained. For instance, the way in which potential is hidden was discussed and how to generally unlock it was illustrated, but no suggestions were given to help you find specific kinds of potential for specific needs. This was completely intentional. This book was written in such a way as to help move you toward the perceptual mode of the natural self and allow you to start to perceive with resonance and emerging awareness. I could not and should not attempt to tell you what will come through the doorway of the natural self for you, as I truly cannot know. I can only tell you that it is there and illustrate the basic principles of how it operates.

Let me say one final time that this book has been as simple as we could make it because the subject is simple. This does not in any way take away from the profound opportunities for growth available through the natural self. It is simply the case that no teacher, preacher, guru or mysterious symbol is necessary for your development in every way. Your natural self is the ultimate and most intimate guide to your growth, participation and fulfillment in life. As your natural self, the natural world around you will feed you and blossom through you, and you will find truth, your voice, your place, fulfillment, and more than you could ever imagine.

Glossary

Abstraction:
A reference to something else with a symbol or even a feeling of some sort. Abstractions include, but are definitely not limited to, thoughts, ideas, words, rules, laws, names, structures, measurements, images, symbols, beliefs, values, expectations, signs, anger, shame, resentment, jealousy, fear, irritation and blame.

Emerging Awareness:
The arising of understanding within consciousness without extracting meaning from abstractions or using reasoning. It is one of two important aspects of the perceptual mode of the natural self.

False Self:
A collection of abstractions about one's self that we mistake to be the real self, the natural self. The false self obscures the natural self and thus obscures our relationship with the natural world and our potential for learning from it, finding what we are capable of and contributing what we are capable of.

False World:

A collection of abstractions about reality that obscures the natural world and gives us the false impression that we are separated from reality. The false world is championed by the culture we live within.

Natural Self:

The real self, the self that exists naturally and is revealed when we let go of our attachment to the false self. All of our potential lives in the natural self.

Natural World:

Everything that surrounds the natural self without the abstractions that constitute the false world. The natural world is the foundation of life and the source of our fulfillment by participating in it.

Reality:

In this book we typically use this word as synonymous with the natural world. We do not use it to mean "reality as the situation describes." Reality is what it is—you simply have to let go of what you have been told it is to experience it.

Resonance:

The sense of understanding and learning what is real from what is not real, as well as feeling flows and blocks in one's own connection to the natural world, and as experienced by actively or passively orienting to it. It is one of two important aspects of the perceptual mode of the natural self.

Final Acknowledgment

For those who felt the acknowledgments at the front of the book were more than enough, this last part won't mean much. But for those who understand the potentially powerful cauldrons of growth that relationships of all sorts *can* be and who understand the depth that cooperation can bring, these final words may mean everything.

From my wife, Sierra, who is my partner in everything:

Although I did not write this book, I participated in the process and feel that the synergy between Anton and me, along with both our individual and shared experiences throughout the seasons of our lives, led us to a moment in which we experienced our natural selves in the natural world—and named that path Intuisdom.

From that moment, we knew our lives were forever changed and that Anton *had* to write the book—though we both knew that, like fulfillment, it could not be forced. The book is simple and was written as naturally as it came.

Life is intertwined with the changing tides and waves that the vast, constant and rhythmic sea produces and through the crash and current of each wave I have fallen, learned, loved, lost and come to know through experience that I did not get up all by myself. There were family, friends and teachers who left an imprint on my soul and in the sand along the shoreline of my life whom I am honored to have the opportunity to acknowledge.

To nature—my first teacher. There are no words, but instead many smells, beauty, appreciation and memories that have taken me to places and done more for me than any human being. I remain in awe.

To Anton—my husband and partner through the raging storms at sea and the calmness of the moonlit shore. I thank you for it all—as it is what has brought us to this moment.

To my mother—who demonstrated what perseverance is—I am so grateful and love you so much. To Matz—your love and devotion to our family is immeasurable. To my siblings, Debbie, Greg, Karen and Michael—my first best friends—I love you all. To my nieces and nephews—Leslie, Laurie, Ritter, Anjelica, Morgan and Major—all of whom continue to remind me of what simple joy is.

To Doug Wilson, who taught me that love and loss are only a beginning for so much more to come. Oh, the aches and lessons of the heart that lead to other paths on this journey that may not otherwise have been taken. I miss you and I thank you.

To Kathy "Mertie" Sokol for a 30-year friendship that can't be compared to any other—for there is no other like this one. You are so much to me. Thank you.

To my teachers and friends I've learned from along the way: Guru Simran, Shabad, Laura Kamm, Jerome Downs, K.C. Miller, Joan Anderson, Lorrie Caplan-Shern, Carrie Newell, Joe Oviedo, Susan Lorentzen, Mel & Mary Rose, Paul Rose, Mari Tautimes, Robbie & Steve Gillean, David Taylor, Marcy Randolph, Lynda & Phil Randolph, Agnes Harris, Gwynda Holemon, Barbara O'Reagan, Helen Stone and Roy Krause. Thank you for your contributions to my life. I remain so thankful.

To end, I wish to share something Anton wrote to me a few years ago and I hope in some way it speaks to you, the reader, as significantly as it spoke to me.

"In this world of ours with struggle and pain seeming to invade every breath, it is so very important to uncover and recognize, as well as to outright create, pearls and treasures of consciousness, support, validation, growth, love, and simple acknowledgment of others in every moment available…and then to expand those moments into minutes, hours, days and even years of happiness and fulfillment."

Sometimes the simplest things are the very things that can forever change our lives and the planet.

~Sierra Byers, September 2009